DARK SIDE OF THE MOON

First published in 2000 by Franklin Watts
A division of the Watts Publishing Group Limited
96 Leonard Street, London EC2A 4XD

Editor in Chief: John C. Miles
Designer: Jason Anscomb
Consultant: Robin Kerrod

A CIP catalogue record for this book
is available from the British Library.

ISBN   0 7496 3468 5 (hbk)
         0 7496 3472 3 (pbk)

Printed in Great Britain

DARK SIDE OF THE MOON

BY
MICHAEL JOHNSTONE

ILLUSTRATIONS
BY ANDY DIXON

W
FRANKLIN WATTS
NEW YORK • LONDON • SYDNEY

CHANGE IS A CONSTANT

Let's step back in time for a moment –
to the very beginning of the twentieth century.
In the United States, Orville and Wilbur Wright were
convinced they could take to the air in a mechanically powered
aircraft. But they hadn't achieved it yet.
In Russia, an obscure scientist called Konstantin Tsiolkovsky had been
working on the theory of rocket space flight for a few years. But to
most people the idea that one day men and women would live and
work in space was pie in the sky.
The motor car had been invented, but the few cars on the roads in
Europe and the United States belonged to the very rich.
Nuclear power hadn't been thought of.

•

Let's come up to date.
Every minute of every day a jet aircraft takes off to carry cargo
and passengers for hundreds, even thousands of kilometres.
Men and women have lived and worked for months at a time in
orbiting space stations. Twelve men have walked on the Moon.
In the developed world, life without a motor car would be
unthinkable for millions.
A few nuclear bombs could wipe out civilization as we know it.
Given the way technology has altered our lives in the past century,
it's hard to imagine what's going to happen in the next.

•

Or is it?
In the United States, scientists at NASA – the
National Aeronautics and Space Administration – are hard at work
developing new technology. Technology that will make it possible for
us to live and work on the Moon, to travel to Mars, to send manned
missions to other parts of our solar system and one day, perhaps,
beyond it. So let's step into the future, enjoy an adventure set at the
end of the twenty-first century, and then learn a little about
what tomorrow's world may be like.

DARK SIDE OF THE MOON

'David, aren't you ready yet?' The strain Mary Evans had been working under since the troubles broke out was obvious from the tension in her voice. David listened to it echo round the spartan room that had been his sleeping quarters during his stay on the Moon and felt sorry for her.

'Coming, Mom,' he replied. 'Just got to download some statistics from the main computer onto my micro. I'll be ten minutes.'

'Be here in five! I'm on my way to the cardrome. And I haven't got much time. You know how things are!'

Parents! Who needs them? sighed David as he slid his micro into the transfer drive and walked around the room picking up the last of his things, stuffing them higgledy-piggledy into his bag, then telling the main computer which files he wanted to take back to Earth with him.

As he waited for ELVIS to find the files on the main drive and transfer them to his micro he sighed again, irritated that his trip had been cut short by two weeks.

It had passed in a flash.

Had it really been only four weeks since his father had seen him off . . . ?

* * * * *

'See you in six weeks,' said David Tang Snr, leaning forward to kiss his son goodbye a few moments after the final boarding call for the Spacebus flight had rasped round the departure lounge.

Normally, only passengers and crew were allowed in the departure lounge, but when you are the son of one of the major players in world affairs, it's amazing how rigid rules can be relaxed. Drawing away from the older man, David Jnr thought *Being kissed by your father is OK when you are a kid, but when you're fourteen – come on!*

The black-haired youth held out his hand. 'See you, Dad,' he said gruffly.

Father and son were so alike that the last passengers scurrying to get to the departure gate in time turned and stared.

The older man smiled, shook his son's hand and clapped him on the shoulder. 'Give your mother a kiss from me,' he smiled.

'Sure!'

'And stay out of trouble!'

'Dad!'

A few minutes later David was making his way along the glass jetway towards the spacecraft. Through transparent walls he could see the waiting transporter. Wisps of vapour rose from the fuel tanks as the ultra-cold liquid propellants inside chilled the cowling. This gave the spaceship a mysterious, almost sinister appearance.

'Welcome aboard Spacebus *US Grant*,' the friendly flight attendant smiled at David as he made his way down the central aisle. 'Do you know your seat number?'

'12B,' said David, taking in the name embroidered into her one-piece spacesuit – Rachel Ashford – and beneath it, Senior Flight Attendant.

The attractive redhead squeezed the electronic pad in her hand.

'You must be David Tang.'

David nodded.

'First trip to the Moon, isn't it?'

'Yes. But I've been in a Spacebus before.'

'When was that?'

'Last year. Dad had to go to a conference in the Heavyside Hilton and he took Mom and me along. It was wonderful.'

'I'm sure it was,' Rachel laughed. 'It's the best space hotel in orbit. Anyway,' she went on, 'if you've been on a Spacebus before, you'll know all about take-off procedure, then?'

'Sure,' David buckled himself into his seat. 'Dad insisted I went on pre-flight training both times.'

'Young lady,' someone in the seat behind David said, 'I can't seem to get the hang of this thing.'

'See you later, David,' Rachel said, and a few moments later he heard her tell whoever had spoken that he was trying to fasten his wife's seat belt buckle into his own shoulder harness.

'Hey!' the man said a second or so later. 'Isn't that – er – what's his name?'

'Who?' a woman's voice asked.

'The guy who got a life sentence yesterday. For terrorism and kidnapping. And extortion.'

David looked up and instantly recognized the tall, long-haired man being led down the aisle by two burly security guards.

'Sergio Ceraulo!' the woman gasped. 'So it is. What's he doing on this Spacebus?'

'Being taken to Nixon Pen, I suppose,' the man said. 'That new high-security prison on the Moon. Security there's tighter than a miser's purse strings. That's where all terrorists are being sent these days.'

As Ceraulo passed David's aisle seat he caught the boy staring at the steel rings circling each wrist and connected to each other by a solid steel bar.

'Got a problem, kid?' he snapped.

'Shut up, Ceraulo,' barked the front guard. 'Shut up and keep walking. We've got a compartment all to ourselves right at the back.'

'Yeah! Just the three of us,' wheezed the second guard. 'Ain't that cosy?'

David turned in his chair and watched Ceraulo being marched down the aisle. He was just about to look away when the gangster looked back and shot him a glance that sent a shiver of fear running down the boy's spine.

Somehow, in that instant, David knew that their paths would cross again. And when they did, there was going to be trouble.

CHAPTER 2

'Cabin staff to take-off positions,' a voice crackled down the intercom.

'Hurry up, Ceraulo,' rasped the guard bringing up the rear and prodding the master-criminal in the back. 'You're keeping these nice people waiting.'

David settled back in his seat, waiting for the jolt that would tell him the pilot had released the brakes and the Spacebus was about to lumber into life.

As the *US Grant* taxied up the runway, the small video screen staring at David from the back of the seat in front began to glow and the same friendly face that had greeted him aboard began to talk the passengers through take-off, in-flight and safety procedures.

No sooner had she finished than David felt as if a giant hand was pushing him back in his seat. With a deafening roar the Spacebus began to gather speed at a dizzying rate and thundered down the runway.

Looking out of the porthole, everything on the Earth began to appear smaller and smaller, the traffic on the eighteen-lane California Freeway soon looking like lines of ants scuttling along the pages of a small-scale street map before vanishing altogether.

'You can open your eyes now, Thelma,' the man behind said a few minutes later. 'We're off.'

'I know space travel is meant to be safer than – '

'Ssh!' her husband shushed her. 'Here's the captain.'

'Good morning, ladies and gentlemen,' said the craggy, good-looking man whose face now filled the video screen. 'I'm Captain Tom Parker-Lee and I'd like to welcome you aboard LuftLunar Flight LL865 to the Armstrong Lunar Space Terminal.

'Those of you sitting on the left now have a memorable view of the entire San Francisco Bay area and a few minutes from now you should be able to see right down the coast to Los Angeles.'

'Fred!' David heard the woman say. 'Tell that space waitress we want to change seats. I wanna see LA.'

'Don't be silly, Thelma.' Fred sounded as if he was trying to soothe a two-year-old. 'And don't call the cabin crew space waitresses. It's rude.'

' – up to 30,000 kilometres an hour, giving us a flight time of thirteen hours and an estimated time of arrival of 22.00 hours Western Seaboard Time,' the Captain went on. 'In the meantime, sit back, relax and enjoy the flight.'

All the time the Captain had been talking, the speed registering on the Machometer alongside the video screen had been increasing. It now showed that the spacecraft was shooting through the atmosphere high above the Earth at over Mach 1, more than the speed of sound.

Beneath the Machometer, the constantly changing numbers on an altimeter showed the height the US Grant was reaching. On the large screens set above the aisles every four or five rows, David could see the west coast of the United States getting farther and farther away with each second that passed.

He had tried to sound cool when he had told Rachel that this wasn't his first space trip, but he found it hard to control his excitement as the jet engines' whine gave way to a muffled roar and the booster rockets took over.

'What's happening, Fred?' Thelma screeched.

'The air outside is too thin for the standard jet engines to operate,' Fred shouted. 'The booster's got much more powerful engines. They generate enough thrust to keep us going as well as pushing us out of the Earth's atmosphere after take-off. That's all.'

'All? That noise is going right through my head.'

'Thelma!' Fred sounded as if he was speaking through clenched teeth. 'Shut up!'

On the large screens, the pictures of the horizon began to show the definite curve of the Earth's rim. And a few moments later, when the Spacebus was at 30,500 metres, David's stomach began to flutter with excitement. The sky changed colour from the sort of deep blue you only ever see above mountain-top ski resorts on a late, sunlit afternoon to the velvety blackness of infinite space.

Looking around, David could see that he wasn't the only one who was feeling as if his body had taken on a mind of its own and was pushing against his harness, trying to float off his seat.

'I don't like this, Fred,' Thelma moaned.

'Thelma – '

Before Fred could finish whatever it was he had been going to say, a dull rumbling rose from underneath the *US Grant,* sending a shudder the length of the cabin.

A second later Thelma's scream almost drowned out an ear-splitting roar that was louder than a thousand raging rhinoceroses on the rampage.

CHAPTER 3

'Shut up, Thelma!' Fred yelled at the top of his voice as the *US Grant* started to tilt upwards, thrusting the passengers back in their seats. 'It's routine. Weren't you paying any attention to the pre-take-off video?'

David smiled to himself, remembering how scared he had been when exactly the same thing had happened on his first journey into space. He had known that the rumble was simply the sound of hydraulic jacks raising the Spacebus to separation position. And he had been aware that the roar came from the Spacebus's engines being fired just before booster and 'bus separated, the first to return automatically to Earth to be refuelled and used over and over again, the second to continue on its journey into space.

Once again Rachel Ashford's face appeared on the video screen. 'Ladies and gentlemen, the Captain has now switched off the Fasten Seat Belts sign. But as we are in zero gravity, we recommend that you keep them fastened. Should you decide to leave your seat, please remember to grasp the handholds as you were taught at pre-flight training sessions – '

'What pre-flight training sessions?' David heard Fred behind him say.

'I forgot to tell you about them,' bleated his wife.

'Thelma!'

'– and enjoy the rest of your flight.'

'Fabulous, isn't it?' The man beside David spoke for the first time. 'Looking down at the Earth from this height. It's beautiful.'

'Beats virtual reality space flight any day,' David agreed.

'On vacation?' said the man. 'Peter Reynolds, by the way.'

'Yeah. I'm going to stay with my mom. She works for Midway Mining. I'm David – '

'Drink, David?' Rachel Ashford interrupted him before he could tell Peter Reynolds his last name.

'Tab Light, please,' said David.

'Mr Reynolds?'

'Alcohol-free Chardonnay with a dash of elderflower,' Peter Reynolds smiled. 'Then your mother and I are going to be colleagues. I've just been appointed Assistant Chief Executive. She'll be working for me.'

'No, you'll be working for her, Mr Reynolds.' There was a note of pride in David's voice. 'She's MM's Chief Executive, Lunar Operations.'

'Wow! Better watch what I say, then.' The smile widened to a broad grin. 'And it's Peter, please. Don't suppose you play Hourglass Chess, do you?'

'Sure,' David nodded.

'It's on Channel 85,' said Rachel, handing the two of them their drinks.

'Thanks,' they said at the same time, before Peter

added, 'Want a game?'

'Yup! What level?'

'How good are you?'

David shrugged his shoulders. 'Average,' he said modestly.

Peter laughed. 'People who say they're average are usually red hot.'

'Let's play at Level 5 and take it from there,' David suggested.

'Fine by me,' said Peter, as they both opened their armrests and entered 85 on the keyboard that rose from within.

The same image appeared on both screens: two

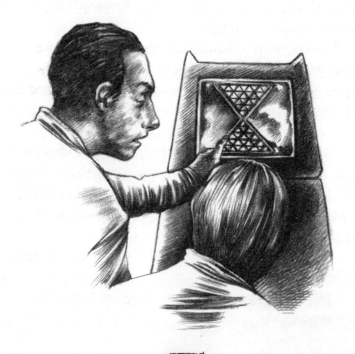

three-dimensional, blunted triangles, one on top of the other and touching at the narrowest point. Inside each were lines of smaller 3D triangles, and at either end, inside the two layers closest to the base, the pieces were lined up.

Images of a clenched fist appeared on either side of the hourglass shape that had given the game its name.

'Right or left?' Peter said.

Peter thought for a second then keyed in R and instantly the right-hand fist opened, revealing a king.

'You go first,' said Peter. 'I'll play down.'

Minutes later the two were engrossed in the game, moving their pieces through the endlessly spinning maze of triangles.

It was soon obvious from the way Peter and David manoeuvred their pieces that both usually played way above Level 5. Hours later, by the time the Captain announced they would soon be coming in to land, neither had outwitted the other.

'Wow!' said the flight attendant who came to make sure their seats were in landing position. 'Level 10! You guys must have IQs way up in the hundreds. Want me to download that for you so you can finish the game later?'

'Thanks,' said David, smiling. 'I've got him on the run at last.'

'In your dreams, sunshine,' laughed Peter. 'In your dreams.'

David looked up at the large video screens, now showing the Moon's surface getting slowly nearer and nearer. At first it looked like a much-used, grey pin-cushion, dotted here and there with occasional tiny spots of green, which only emphasized the greyness of the monochrome landscape.

As the Spacebus closed in, what had looked like pinpricks and pinheads were seen to be deep craters and barren hilltops. What had seemed to be strands of cotton wool widened into dry ravines. Specks of green mushroomed into the man-made, plant-filled biospheres they were – vast pressurised domes with independent air supplies, inside which human beings could live and work as if they were on Earth.

Like all fourteen-year-olds, David liked to think he was cool, but he could do nothing to stop his stomach churning with excitement as the Spacebus got lower and lower.

'I can't wait to get down there,' he thought, thinking of all the things he wanted to do and see.

He wouldn't have been quite so keen if he had known what lay in store for him.

CHAPTER 4

'Ladies and gentlemen,' Rachel Ashford smiled from the video screen, 'we will shortly be landing at Armstrong Lunar Base. Please make sure your seats are in landing position and your seatbelts and harnesses securely fastened. When we are on the runway, please remain in your seats until the Spacebus has come to a halt and the Captain has switched off the Fasten Seat Belts sign.'

'How many times have I heard that?' Peter wondered aloud.

The video screens flickered for a moment before a cockpit-eye-view of the lunar landing strip appeared, stretching as far as the eye could see.

'Here we go,' said Peter as a heavy clanking announced that the landing gear doors had opened and the enormous wheels had dropped into position.

A few minutes later there was a jolt as the wheels came into contact with the runway and reinforced rubber spun against reinforced concrete.

'Our Father –' David heard Thelma begin.

The rest of her prayer was drowned out by a loud splintering followed a second later by a blood-curdling scream.

A hundred heads shot round to see what on Earth was happening.

'How the – ' gasped David.

'I don't believe it,' breathed Peter.

'Fred!' moaned Thelma.

For there, framed in the shattered doorway, stood Sergio Ceraulo, Rachel Ashford between his arms, the solid metal bar of his handcuffs pressing hard into her neck.

'Do what I say,' he shouted, 'or I'll break her windpipe.'

Nobody moved a muscle as Sergio Ceraulo forced the terrified woman down the aisle, making her grip one handhold after another to stop them floating upwards.

'Out of the way,' barked Ceraulo to the two flight attendants blocking the aisle just behind David.

One of the attendants moved as if he was about to try to spring forwards.

'I meant what I said,' snarled Ceraulo, pulling the metal bar so hard on Rachel's throat that she wheezed horribly as she desperately tried to breathe some air into her lungs.

The two attendants squeezed themselves to either side of the aisle to let Ceraulo and his petrified hostage pass.

'Fred!' Thelma moaned moments after kidnapper and hostage had passed David's seat. 'I think I'm gonna throw up!'

Across from him, David saw the passenger on the aisle seat open the briefcase on his lap, the noise of the engines drowning the click of the catches.

'What the – ' Peter breathed as the man took out a syringe and a phial of clear liquid.

Peter and David watched intently as the man inserted the point of the needle into the phial, then withdrew the plunger, drawing whatever was in the phial into the syringe.

As quickly as he could do it with one hand, the man unbuckled his seat belt and shoulder harness, stood up and moved silently towards Ceraulo.

'What's he doing?' yelled Thelma.

In a flash, Ceraulo turned and as he did so a terrible rasping rose in Rachel's throat and her hands shot to the metal bar, desperately trying to stop it cutting deep into her larynx.

The criminal and the terrified woman began to move towards the front of the cabin. The metal bar scraped up Rachel's throat to her chin, jerking her head violently backwards.

'He's going to break her neck,' gasped Peter.

The rasping had turned into a desperate choking sound and Rachel's pale skin was beginning to turn blue when the man creeping towards Ceraulo and the dying woman flexed his legs against an empty seat and bounded towards them, his syringe pointing at the terrorist.

David saw the needle pierce Ceraulo's pale blue one-piece flightsuit.

Instantly the criminal's body shuddered as if a thousand volts were shooting through it and he collapsed in a heap.

'Yes!' someone behind David shouted.

'Look at her,' someone else yelled. 'She looks as if she's dead.'

'Oh no,' wept Thelma as eager hands freed the

apparently lifeless young woman and pulled her onto the floor, leaving Ceraulo where he was.

'Leave him,' said the doctor who had rescued Rachel, kneeling over her and bringing the palms of both hands down hard on her chest. 'He's not going anywhere. There was enough in that syringe to knock out a herd of elephants.'

Gently he opened the girl's mouth, covered it with his own and breathed into it.

'Come on,' he said through clenched teeth as he raised his head and brought his hands down on her chest again.

'Thank you! Thank you!' he cried as Rachel groaned slightly and her shoulders heaved as her eyelids fluttered open.

'What –' she croaked, her left hand rubbing the angry-looking red mark on her neck.

'Just stay where you are,' said her saviour. 'You're going to be all right.'

But Rachel raised herself on one arm. Seeing Ceraulo slumped further down the aisle, she fell back to the floor in a dead faint.

CHAPTER 5

'What in the name of the Man in the Moon's been going on?' Mary Evans wanted to know after David had hugged her and kissed her twice.

'First one's from me,' he said. 'The second's from Dad.'

'Three men have just come through on stretchers,' David's mother said. 'And a terrified-looking flight attendant with a nasty mark on her neck has just been pushed into security in a wheelchair.'

'That was Rachel Ashford – she was almost murdered by that terrorist guy, Sergio what's-his-name – '

'Ceraulo,' said Mary. 'I heard he's going to serve his sentence at Nixon.'

'Twenty years!' David nodded.

'What happened to him on board?' Mary asked.

'He managed to overpower one of the guards', David answered, 'when he got up to pee. And the other one when he came out of the bathroom, apparently. That's who the three on the stretchers were. Ceraulo and the guys meant to be guarding him.'

'Well, he won't be able to do that at Nixon. Thank goodness,' said Mary. 'Security there's – '

'Tighter than a miser's purse strings,' said David,

remembering what he'd heard said earlier.

'Come on,' Mary said, taking David's arm. 'Let's get your things. My new Prover's outside.'

'You never told me you had a pressurized moon rover,' said David. 'Can I drive it?'

'In your dreams, David,' laughed his mother, flicking a lock of hair from her eyes. 'In your dreams.'

'You're the second person who's said that to me today,' David said as mother and son walked to the baggage carousel.

'Who was the first?'

'Your new Assistant Chief Executive – '

'When did you meet him?' asked Mary.

'He was on the Spacebus,' said David. 'We played Hourglass Chess all the way here. He's a great player.'

'He's a late, great player,' laughed Mary. 'He was due here yesterday.'

'There he is.' David pointed to Peter, who was standing by the conveyor belt waiting for his luggage.

'No it's not,' said Mary, looking at the dumpy man with the bald head standing at the end of the carousel. 'Not unless he's put on fifty pounds and shrunk since his assessment.'

'Not him!' said David, nodding towards the man at the other side of the belt. 'Him. The fat guy's called Fred something.'

'Looks like the sort of tourist who'd be happier at SaharaDisney,' said Mary, walking towards Peter Reynolds, arm outstretched ready to shake his hand.

'Peter!' Mary, with David just behind her, approached the tall, broad-shouldered man who turned and smiled.

'Hi, David,' he said, tapping a pocket on his flightsuit. 'We must finish that game.'

'This is – ' began David.

'We know each other,' his mother smiled at Peter. 'How did the meeting go?'

Peter frowned and David saw him glance in his direction.

'It's all right,' Mary said. 'We brought David up never to repeat anything he heard about his father's or my work. Right, David?'

He nodded.

'So?' Mary looked quizzically at her new Number Two.

'Well, did you know there was another attack on an MM installation?' he asked. 'This time in Luzon.'

'In the Philippine Confederation,' Mary said.

'Ten out of ten for geography,' said David, then seeing the look his mother shot at him, wished he had stayed quiet.

'The politics of the whole area is one of my speciality subjects,' Peter went on. 'That's why the Board asked me to attend their meeting yesterday. To give my assessment of the situation.'

'Of course,' said Mary. 'I'd forgotten you were an authority on Pacific Ocean countries.'

'There's been nothing about any attacks on MM installations in the papers,' interrupted David, who was an avid reader of the world's press. 'Are they orchestrated?

'I think it's time we got you to my quarters,' said Mary, then she turned to Peter and asked, 'Can you fill me in on the details in my office first thing in the morning?'

Peter nodded.

'But, Mom,' David protested. 'This is just getting interesting.'

'I think you'll find what's outside a great deal more interesting,' Mary laughed. 'Come on.'

'Wow!' gasped David when he saw the transporter waiting for them outside the terminal building. 'She's a beaut!'

'After you,' smiled Mary, stepping to one side so that David would reach the gleaming silver Prover before she did. 'Passenger seat,' she called after him.

'Mo-om!'

'Passenger seat,' she said again firmly.

David was about half a metre from the car when suddenly the doors opened, flipping silently upwards before coming to rest on the roof, making the Prover look like a bird about to soar into the air.

'A Gullwing,' he gasped, spinning around, an unspoken question on his face.

'It generates its own forcefield,' said Mary, knowing what he was about to ask. 'When that's broken by someone it's been programmed to recognize, the doors open automatically.'

'How's it been programmed to recognize me?' David asked. 'I've only just got here.'

Mary grinned then said, 'I got your father to send me a sample of your DNA.'

'So that's what he wanted it for!' said David. 'He said it was for school security.'

'You ain't seen nothing yet,' Mary said, imitating Al Jolson, a famous film actor from the early days of the movies.

As his mother got into the driver's seat, David admired the glowing instrument panel.

He was just about to ask what all the dials were when a voice floated out of the tiny speaker so unexpectedly that he almost jumped out of his skin. 'Welcome to the Moon, David!' the voice said.

'What? Who?' croaked the astonished boy.

'Say hello to Gladys!' Mary was clearly enjoying showing off her new car to her son.

'Gladys?'

'I had to call her something!'

'You mean this car – this beautiful piece of machinery – is called Gladys?'

'Yup!' giggled Mary, then, seeing Peter Reynolds climb into a waiting lunar taxi, she said, 'I should have offered him a lift. Hope he doesn't think I'm rude.'

'Power source?' Gladys's tinny voice made David jump again.

'Electromagnetic.' Mary said the word so slowly and deliberately she sounded like a robot.

'Route?'

'LH 3 until we leave the Armstrong Biosphere at Airlock 10 – '

'LH?' said David.

'Lunar Highway,' said Mary.

'And after we leave the biosphere?' Gladys wanted to know.

'Airlock?' David wanted to know.

'All biospheres are filled with pressurized air,' explained Mary. 'Airlocks allow us to go in and out of them without affecting the pressure inside.'

'And after we leave the biosphere?' Gladys asked again.

'There's nothing new about them,' Mary went on. 'Airlocks, that is.'

'Could someone please tell me where you want me to go after we leave the biosphere?'

She sounds annoyed, thought David. *Gladys actually sounds annoyed.*

'Switch to solar power, manual control,' Mary said. 'I want to show David some of the sights on the way to the MM complex. Probably go off-track.'

'Understood!' said Gladys. 'Thank you!'

'Looking for something?' Mary asked, seeing her son fumbling around the side of his seat.

'Seat belt?'

'Aren't any.'

'But if we're going out of the biosphere, how about zero gravity?' said David. 'Won't I float up?'

'No,' explained Mary. 'There is some gravity here. About a sixth of what it is on Earth. So you weigh about ten kilos. And anyway, Provers are pressurized, remember?'

'But what if we crash?' said David.

'Ssh!' smiled his mother. 'Gladys will hear you.' With a slight hum, the Prover moved from the parking bay and slid into the stream of traffic winding its way from the Base.

'The three inside lanes are all on automatic like us,' said Mary. 'The distance between each car is strictly controlled. No chance of a crash.'

'How about the outside two lanes?'

'They're for drivers on manual. "Accident alleys" they're called.'

'How big is it?' David asked. 'The Armstrong Biosphere.'

'It covers about 15 square kilometres,' said Mary. 'It's one of the biggest.'

'Who owns them all?' David wanted to know.

'A few are privately owned by individuals. But most are owned by governments or huge multinationals like MM. But why all these questions? Don't they teach you anything in school these days?'

'Sure,' said David. 'But seeing the biospheres from

space and actually being in one is so different from reading about them. I mean the light, for instance – '

'You'd never think it was artificial, would you?' Mary said. 'They've got it just right.'

'Approaching Airlock 10,' Gladys announced, slowing down and moving into the exit lane.

'Thanks, Gladys,' said Mary. 'I'll go on manual now.'

The Prover lurched slightly as Mary pressed the pedal by her left foot.

'Oops!' sighed Gladys.

'Sorry,' Mary said. 'Haven't quite got it yet.'

The bright overhead light dimmed as Mary steered Gladys into the mouth of the tunnel right ahead, the sign *Air Lock 10 – Get in Lane* flashing brightly above it.

No sooner had the back of the Prover passed underneath the sign than there was a soft swish as a sheet of green see-through material slid down from the roof, sealing the car in the air lock.

'Now what?' David wondered aloud.

'We'll drive to the other end of the tunnel, go through the barrier there and – '

The rest of what she said was drowned out by the deafening sound of a siren from behind.

David twisted around in his seat.

'Look out, Mom!' he screamed. 'There's a van right behind us and unless someone jams on the brakes it's going to ram right into us!'

Mary Evans pulled the steering wheel so hard to the left that, had it not been for the electromagnets keeping his flightsuit firmly in place, David would have been thrown from his seat as the van, its siren still wailing, roared past.

'Not so hard, please,' intoned Gladys.

'Sorry!' said Mary, struggling to get the Prover under control. 'I had to act fast to get out of the way of that blasted van.'

'Its details have been registered in my computer,' David could have sworn there was a smug tone in Gladys's voice, 'if you wish to report the driver to the police.'

'Gladys, that *was* the police,' said Mary, steering her car back on track. 'Well, the security guards from Nixon Pen at any rate.'

'The number wasn't registered as a security transporter.' This time David could have sworn Gladys sounded sulky!

'They certainly were in a hurry,' he said, relaxing in his seat.

'So would you be if you'd got one of the most dangerous men in the world in the back,' said Mary. 'They won't ease up until they've got him firmly under lock and key, just in case.'

'Just in case what?' asked David.

'In case someone tries to spring him.'

'On the Moon?'

'David,' said Mary, pressing her foot on the brake to slow Gladys down as she approached Airlock 10's outer door. 'That man is like a spider in the middle of a web that stretches from Manila to Mars.'

As she spoke Mary steered her Prover into one of the lines of security booths at the end of the tunnel. As the window by her side slid down soundlessly, she reached out, tapped a number into the line of keys below a small patch of dark glass fixed to the booth wall and then pressed the pad of her thumb against it.

Almost at once, a green light flashed overhead and seconds later Mary turned to David and said, 'Want to see something of the Moon?'

'Lead on,' said David. 'Sorry, make that drive on.'

David had seen pictures of the lunar landscape, of course. And the lunar section of his local virtual reality centre was one of his favourite haunts. But nothing he had seen there was quite like what he was looking at now.

He remembered from history that when Buzz Aldrin, one of the first two men to land on the Moon more than 120 years before, was asked what it was like there, he had described the lunar scene as 'magnificent desolation'.

The road they were on stretched straight ahead as far as the eye could see, narrowing to a pinprick on the horizon. On either side the land looked like a vast luminous desert, pitted with craters and scattered with large boulders and smaller rocks scattered here and there, as if a giant's game of marbles had been interrupted.

Far to the right, a range of mountains rose into the pitch black sky and to the left David could just make out what seemed to be a blob of blue plastic.

'What's that?' he asked his mother.

'The Lunar Apennines,' said Mary.

'No, not the mountains,' said David. 'I know what they are. We're in the Sea of Showers, aren't we?'

'My! Who's been brushing up on his lunar geography?' laughed Mary. 'And if you want to be precise, it's *Mare Imbrium*. We use Latin names here.'

'*Questum objectum sinister?*' David said in bad schoolboy Latin.

'Sorry?'

'What's the thing on my left? I thought you said you used Latin here.'

'I didn't know you spoke Latin.'

'I don't yet.' David shrugged his shoulders. 'Not properly. But I think I want to be a doctor when I leave school. Dad said if I was serious I should start Latin. And even if I change my mind it will still come in handy if I ever decide to learn early European languages.'

'I hope you're keeping up your Japanese and your Mandarin. You know how important China is now.'

'Mo-om! I've been taking Mandarin since kindergarten,' sighed David. 'Now are you going to tell me what that blue thing is over there?'

'The Apollo Museum,' Mary said, glancing to her left. 'It's on the list of "must-do's" I had my secretary prepare for you. It's fabulous. It's got a lot of the equipment used in the early days of lunar exploration.'

'Is the US flag there?' David wanted to know. 'The one the first men on the Moon stuck in the ground.'

'No, that's still where they left it!' said Mary. 'It's the most popular tourist attraction on the Moon. Wanna go see it?'

'Now?'

'Why not?' Mary grinned then leaned forward a little and said, 'Gladys. What's the shortest route to Old Glory Park from here?'

'Turn off at Junction 4, follow MLH6 until you get to the Lyndon Johnson Turnoff and it's 8.65 kilometres down LB-W 8.'

'Thank you, Gladys,' said Mary, then went on for David's benefit, 'That's Minor Lunar Highway and Lunar By-way, before you ask.'

David watched the lunar landscape whizz by as Mary followed Gladys's route to Old Glory Park. 'Not long now,' said Mary about ten minutes after they had turned off the busy main road.

No sooner had she spoken than a red light flashed on the dashboard and Gladys's voice filled the Prover's passenger compartment. 'Please return to your office right away.'

David looked at his mother and saw the frown on her face. 'Something wrong?' he asked.

'Must be,' said Mary. 'That light means there's an alert on!'

CHAPTER 8

'What was it all about, Mom?'

It was the first time David had seen his mother since she had dropped him off at her quarters the evening before and dashed to her office.

'Something's come up on Earth,' said Mary, sipping her coffee. 'Nothing for us worry about really. Now let's see what we've got planned for you today.'

But David knew that his mother was worried about something. 'So why the alert?'

Mary put down her cup. 'Oh, very well,' she said. 'You heard Peter Reynolds talking about MM's installations being attacked by guerrillas?'

David nodded.

'Well, we've found out the government of Y'Altai is sheltering the guerrillas. And the governments that back MM have demanded that the Y'Altais hand them over.'

'Y'Altai?'

'Small republic in southern China. We've got people from Y'Altai and her allies here,' said Mary. 'And people from hostile countries. If there's trouble on Earth, things here could get a bit uncomfortable.'

* * * * *

As the demands and counter-demands flew back and

forth the situation on Earth soon began to get heated despite the efforts of David's father and other senior diplomats to calm things down.

'Do you think David should come home?' Mary asked her husband one night after David had been on the Moon for about two weeks. 'Tourists are leaving.'

'No,' said David Tang. 'Let him stay on. Things should start calming down. How's he doing?'

'He's having a ball,' said Mary. 'He's been all over the place. He loved the new observatory, the Blairdome, so much, he's been back three times.'

'How are things with you?' David asked.

Before Mary could answer, David Jnr burst into the room.

'It's great, Mom,' he cried. 'I think I'm going to study astro-physics when I leave – ' He stopped when he saw his father's face on the screen. 'Hi, Dad,' he smiled. 'How's it going?'

'Fine, son,' said David Snr. 'Just been talking to your mother about the situation here.'

'You don't want me to come home, do you?' David sounded wary. 'Cos if you do – '

'No. You stay put,' said his father. 'We've got everyone around the table at last. They're still talking.'

* * * * *

The first scuffle between Y'Altai Alliance workers and miners from other countries started when one of the robots being operated by a Japanese mechanic accidentally severed a power cable, cutting off electricity to a mine shaft being extended by Y'Altai-controlled robots and trapping twenty Y'Altai engineers in a lift.

When they found out what had happened, the Y'Altais accused the Japanese of deliberately cutting the cable.

Within seconds fists were flying, and by the time security workers broke up the fight, three Y'Altais and two Japanese workers had been badly hurt.

'We'll have to segregate Y'Altai and allied workers from the others,' said Mary to Peter Reynolds when she had read the report. 'Organize it, please.'

* * * * *

The next day, the Y'Altais and their allies walked out of the negotiations on Earth and nothing David Tang Snr could do or say would bring them back.

The day after that, the Y'Altais were given an

ultimatum. Unless they handed over the guerrillas who had been attacking MM installations, random non-nuclear airstrikes would be launched against them.

When the Y'Altais' allies said they would launch counter-attacks, their failure to use the words 'non-nuclear' was widely noted in the world's press.

As the crisis deepened, more and more fights broke out on the Moon and more and more tourists headed for home, fighting one another for places on the already overbooked Spacebuses. Scientists working on lunar research projects were recalled by their governments. Work was halted on building the launch base for missions to Mars and the workers were ferried back to Earth.

'When the next Spacebus leaves,' Peter Reynolds said to David as they were playing hourglass chess one night, 'the only ones left here will be MM people and the security guys at Nixon Pen.'

David was about to say *And the prisoners in Nixon*, when his mother burst into the room.

'Go get packed, David,' she said. 'You're going home immediately.'

'But Dad said it's safer here than on Earth.'

'Things have changed.' Mary was tense. 'Your father's just been on screen. US intelligence has uncovered a Y'Altai plot to launch an attack.'

'What, on the USA?' Peter exclaimed.

'No!' Mary's voice shook. 'On the Moon.'

'Why would they want to attack the Moon?' Peter leaned forward, saved the game and switched off the computer.

'Eutropium supplies,' said Mary.

'Eutropium?' David, who knew all the elements in the Periodic Table, had never heard of the stuff.

'It's a previously unknown element that's just been discovered on the far side of the Moon,' Mary explained. 'A thousand times more radioactive than even the highest-grade plutonium.'

'So they can use it to make nuclear warheads much more cheaply?'

Mary nodded. 'Yup. Goodness knows how they found out about it, but they have.'

'But – '

'David, no more questions. Go and pack.'

'Looks like we're going to have to declare a draw,' said Peter, as David got up to leave the room.

'This series,' smiled David. 'But next time. . .'

'Let's just hope there *is* a next time,' said Mary.

* * * * *

'Operation complete,' the computer's deep, gravelly voice announced a few minutes later.

'Thanks, ELVIS.' David pushed the eject button

and put the micro into his bag with a great deal more care than he had treated his other possessions.

He ran along the passageway and was quite breathless by the time he reached the basement where his mother was waiting. 'And about time too,' she said. 'Come on, we haven't got much time.'

David moved towards the vehicle Mary used to drive around the biosphere. 'No, not that one,' she said. 'We've got to take Gladys.'

'Gladys? But surely you only use that to get from biosphere to biosphere!'

'We've got to get to Ceta 3. The last Spacebus to go from here left three hours ago.'

'But Ceta 3's goodness knows how many kilometres from here!'

'Don't worry. We've got time.'

'Can I take the controls?' Despite his alarm, David still sounded hopeful.

'No!' His mother's voice was stern.

'Oh please, Mom. It's the last chance I'll have to drive one of these babies.'

'Oh, very well,' said Mary.

'I hope you know what you're doing,' Gladys's voice rasped from the sound system as soon as David had sat in the driver's seat.

'Of course I do,' said David. 'Manual control.'

'David!' There was a warning in Mary's voice.

'Sorry, I mean automatic. Power level ten.'

'Power level five is fast enough,' said Mary firmly.

'Will you make up your minds, please,' sighed Gladys. 'Now, route?'

'Route 8 as far as the Tsiolkovsky turn-off then LH 5 to Ceta 3,' David said, and the car moved off.

'There it is,' said Mary after they had been going for about an hour. But before she could point out Ceta 3 to David, a curious clunking came from Gladys's underside. The Prover got slower and slower, then automatically moved onto the hard shoulder before coming to a grinding halt.

'Gladys! What's the matter?' Mary asked.

The only answer she got was a long, low groan.

'Fault Finder,' she said, turning to David.

David touched a panel on the control screen and immediately a diagram of Gladys's various systems appeared on the screen, flashing red at three spots.

'Oh no,' sighed Mary. 'There's a malfunction in the magnetic transformer. I can't fix that. Get the emergency services on the communicator. Give them our position and tell them to be here as soon as possible. I'll raise Ceta 3 and tell them to hold the plane.'

'I'd hate to be your secretary,' said David, pressing the emergency services' number.

Mary turned, smiled at him jokingly and said, 'You're my son. If you were my secretary I'd have said please.'

* * * * *

'They'll be here in thirty minutes.' David turned to his mother who was angrily keying in a number.

'Come on!' she snapped. 'Connect.'

But no matter how many times Mary tried to get through to the number she had for the Ceta 3 Spacebus Centre, there was no response.

'What do we do now?' said David.

'Nothing we can do.' Mary shook her head. 'We're going to miss the Spacebus.'

'I'll get the next one,' said David, shrugging his shoulders.

'There isn't a next one,' said Mary. 'That was the last one out. You're stuck here for the duration.'

'I'd keep out of her way if I were you,' Peter said as he passed David in the corridor three days later. 'To say your mother's in a foul mood's a bit like saying Beijing is the capital of the Chinese Empire.'

'But Beijing *is* the capital of the Chinese Empire,' said David.

'Ever heard of stating the obvious?' grinned Peter. 'See you later.'

'Wish me luck.' David shrugged his shoulders, knocked on the door of his mother's office and went in.

'What do you want, David?' Mary asked, looking up from the screen set in her worktop. 'I'm busy.'

'I know, but – '

'But what?' said Mary.

'The more you interrupt, the longer I'm going to be,' said David in the same cool, logical way his father often used when Mary was irritated, the only thing about her husband she found irritating.

Mary turned from her screen to face her son. 'I just want to know when I'm going home,' David said. 'There's an eclipse of the Sun coming up, and I want to know if I'll be here to watch it.'

Mary ran her hand across her eyebrows. 'Yes, David,' she said wearily. 'You will. There's an embargo on all flights from Earth to the Moon until the crisis is

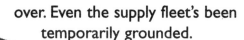

over. Even the supply fleet's been temporarily grounded. Unfortunately.'

'You mean we're running out of food already?' David shook his head in disbelief.

'No!' said Mary. 'But unless this crisis is over quite soon, we could have to start rationing it.'

* * * * *

A week passed with no sign of a solution despite David Tang's round-the-clock efforts to get everyone back to the negotiating table.

On the Moon tempers were starting to fray. Peter Reynolds had, as Mary requested, planned things so that the Y'Altais and their friends had as little contact as possible with miners from other countries. But it was impossible to keep them apart twenty-four hours a day and, when they did meet, the atmosphere was so strained that you could, as Peter commented, slice it with a teaspoon.

'It's going to take one spark and BANG!' he said when he reported to Mary on the tenth day.

'How are supplies?' she asked.

'We're all right for most things . . . ' He stopped and let an unseen word hang in the air.

'But what?' said Mary.

'We're running low on fresh fruit and milk. Stuff like that.' He paused. 'Well, it was fresh a week ago.'

'Why don't you arrange to have it rationed? So much per person per day.'

'They're not going to like that. Especially the Y'Altais. They're vegetarians. The stuff we're short of is vital to their diet.'

'Please do as I say, Mr Reynolds.' Mary's voice was firm.

'Yes, Ma'am!'

* * * * *

The rationing itself didn't cause problems. But when sacks of fruit went missing from a delivery to a mine being worked by Y'Altais a fuse was lit that exploded into violence a few hours later. The furious Y'Altais took to their vehicles and swarmed across the crater they were working in. They attacked a group of Japanese miners surveying a prospective site at the edge of the *Mare Fecundiatis*.

The Japanese stood their ground as best they could but it was hopeless. They were completely outnumbered by seething Y'Altais and helpless to prevent them emptying their precious supply depot.

Worse, before they roared back to base, the

Y'Atlais immobilized the Japanese transporters and put their communicators out of action. This left the surveyors stranded until a search party found them the following day.

Miners from countries friendly to Japan were quick to retaliate, and within days those left on the Moon were on the brink of civil war.

* * * * *

'I don't care if it's the most complete solar eclipse for eight hundred years, never mind eighty. For the tenth time, you are not, repeat not, going to the Blairdome to see it. It's much too dangerous.'

'But, Mom – ' David got no further.

'I said no!' said Mary in a voice that would brook no argument and left the room.

'Yes, Mom! No, Mom! Three bags full, Mom!' he grimaced at the door. 'The Blairdome Observatory is the best place to see that eclipse and the Blairdome Observatory is where I'm going to see it.'

CHAPTER 11

David looked at his watch. Time to go.

No sooner had he pressed the button by the side of the door than it slid silently open and light streamed into his darkened room from the bright corridor beyond.

He stuck his head out as far as he dared and peered out.

Empty.

Clutching his boots, he padded down the corridor, making as little noise as possible.

A sigh of relief rose in his chest when he saw the door to his mother's quarters was firmly closed, but when he was a few metres from the door that led to Peter Reynolds' private office suite his heart leapt into his mouth when he heard it swish open.

An arc of bright light fell on the floor, casting a shadow across the floor and up the wall.

He immediately recognized who it was about to step into the corridor and catch him sneaking out so late at night.

What on earth could he say to her?

Hi, Mom. I was just going to get a glass of water? If his mother swallowed that she'd swallow anything, and despite his apprehension he smiled at the joke he had accidentally made to himself.

Or: *Just going to the bathroom?* If she believed that

she'd believe babies grew on trees.

The moment she saw him standing there in his lunar travel gear, boots in hand, she'd know exactly what he was up to.

He saw the shadow move to come through the doorway, but before his mother stepped into the corridor he heard Peter Reynolds call, 'This needs your signature before you go.'

'Couldn't it wait till morning?' Mary Evans sounded exhausted.

'I'd rather you did it now,' Peter said. 'It's the order for the guards to use stunguns on anyone caught stealing rations.'

'Is it really getting that serious?'

'We're down to a few days' supply of some things, mainly fresh fruit and veg.'

David waited until his mother's shadow vanished then slipped past the door, walked briskly to the stairs and raced to the garage six floors below.

* * * * *

A few minutes later he was sitting astride a high-powered lunar two-wheeler, thundering across the *Mare Nectaris* towards the Blairdome Observatory. But when, an hour later it came into view, in his eagerness to get there he took the next bend far too quickly.

A scream rose in his throat as he lost control

and the lunar landscape seemed to jerk one way then the other before wobbling like a jelly as he parted company with the bike.

'AAAGH!' he cried as he landed about twenty metres from the bike, sending up a cloud of dust.

He lay there for a minute or two, too stunned to move, then clambered to his feet and hobbled back to where the bike lay on its side. But before he got there, three ghostly figures appeared from behind a huge rock by the side of the road.

'Hey, that's my bike!' he shouted as one of the spectres righted the two-wheeler. 'Give it back!'

The figure raised its right arm and the next thing David knew a heavy hand had grabbed his shoulder and spun him round. 'What's going on?' he gasped, staring at the tall figure who had him in his grip.

'Confirm name!' The voice in David's headset had a heavy Y'Altai accent.

'David Tang,' David replied.

'David Tang. Son of Mary Evans. What an excellent hostage you will make.'

'Get your hands off me!' David yelled, but the Y'Altais paid him no attention. He was terrified and well aware that his captors could tell.

With one of them on either side and one behind, he was forced along the highway to where a large transporter was parked by the side of the road. As they approached the back swung open and a small flight of steps automatically uncurled. 'Get in!' he heard someone say.

David clambered aboard and found himself facing a solid sheet of metal less than half a metre away. *There's more room in a can of sardines*, he thought, turning just in time to see the door slam shut in his face, leaving him in complete darkness.

Seconds later, a soft clunk told him the magnetic lock had been activated.

'Let me out!' he cried, thumping on the door.

Suddenly light flooded into the compartment. Turning to face the front, David saw the sheet of metal slide upwards, revealing boxes of supplies piled one on top of the other, nets of vegetables squashed in beside sacks of fruit and more cartons, cans and plastic bottles than he had ever seen before.

A huge blob of red ran down the side of one of the cartons. 'Looks like the tomato ketchup's leaking,' David said aloud, running his finger through the

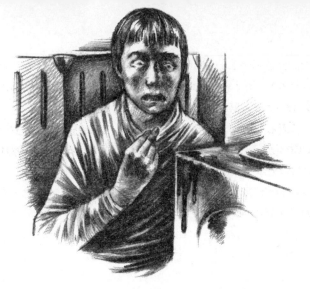

smear. But when he sniffed it, his stomach turned,
and he realized that what he had on his hand
was blood. In his mind's eye he was picturing a band
of miners desperately defending their supplies. His
dark thoughts were interrupted as the engine roared
into life. Caught off guard, David found himself thrown
to one side.

David had had some bumpy rides before, but
never one like this. By the time the transporter came
to a halt an hour later he had been thoroughly
shaken up.

'Get to the back,' a voice crackled through
his headset.

For a moment David thought about hiding among
the crates and sacks but even as the idea flashed into
his head the voice went on, 'And don't try anything
smart. You'll only make things worse for yourself.'

Just as David reached the back door, the sheet of

metal slid down behind him. For a moment he was enveloped in inky darkness before the door opened and he was hauled out.

'OK, OK, OK!' he said. 'I'm not going anywhere.' But despite his protests he was dragged through a doorway and bundled along passageway after passageway before being thrown into a room little bigger than a broom cupboard.

* * * * * *

'Mr Reynolds! My office. Right away!'

Peter Reynolds put down the book he was reading and sighed.

'I'm off duty,' he said to the monitor facing him.

'Please?' The distress on Mary's face was matched by the catch in her voice.

'Right away it is,' he replied, standing up and heading for the door.

'What's the matter?' he said a few moments later when he was facing Mary across her desk.

'This,' she said. 'It was on my voice mail. Listen,' she went on, flicking one of the switches in front of her.

'Message for Mary Evans.' Even the tinny tone couldn't disguise the Y'Altai accent. 'If you care for your son, contact us at 00.30 on Channel 765. Repeat, 00.30 hours on Channel 765.'

'David!' Peter sounded puzzled. 'Where is he?'

'I thought he was in bed,' said Mary. 'But when I went to look . . . I think he must have slipped out and gone to the Blairdome to watch the eclipse.'

'The Blairdome! But that's kilometres from here.'

'There's a lunar two-wheeler missing from the Transporter Pool,' Mary said worriedly. 'What's the time?'

Peter looked at his watch. 'Twenty-past,' he said. 'Ten minutes to go.'

Time had never passed so slowly, or so it seemed to Mary, before the display clicked over to twelve-thirty.

Her hand shook as she turned the channel selector to 765. Almost immediately the screen facing her glowed for a second before David appeared on it, sandwiched between two burly Y'Altai guards.

Before either Mary or Peter could say a word, one of the men read out a list of the food and other supplies they needed. 'Do not try to locate us, or call Security. You will be contacted again in twelve hours with instructions.'

'And if you don't get what you want?' Mary's voice was quiet, but showed no trace of anger or fear. 'If we don't do what you say?'

'We'll kill your son.'

CHAPTER 13

Before Mary or Peter could say another word, the screen went blank.

'Your system's different from mine,' said Peter, gazing at the bank of screens, buttons and switches on Mary's worktop. 'Which is Call Locate?'

Mary's hand flashed across the communication control panel and pressed a small button. 'You tuned into Channel 765 at 00.30. The receiver shielded his location from you.'

'Hardly surprising, is it?' Mary sighed. 'If you've kidnapped someone, you're not exactly going to advertise where you're keeping him, are you?'

'They could be anywhere,' Peter groaned.

'Get on to Security,' Mary said. 'I want every possible place they could be keeping my son searched.'

'You heard what they said about calling Security.'

'Do it, please. I've got to talk to my husband.'

* * * * *

'Hungry?' The Y'Altai standing in the doorway was holding a tray.

David shook his head.

'You haven't eaten any food all day.'

'Not hungry,' David sniffed.

'Suit yourself.' The Y'Altai began to back out.

'Hang on,' said David. 'Eating's not the only thing I haven't done all day. I gotta go and – you know – go.'

'Ah!' A look of comprehension spread across the Y'Altai's face. 'I'll have to take you,' he said, bending down to put the tray on the floor.

Fearful as he was, David saw an opportunity. He sprang forward and kicked the tray out of the Y'Altai's hands.

'Aaagh!' the Y'Altai yelled as a bowl of steaming hot soup shot off the tray and hit him in the face. Quicker than lightning, David ran past him and tried to slam the door, but the Y'Altai was too fast for him.

Despite the hot liquid running down his chin, the Y'Altai threw his weight against the door to keep it open while David on the other side put every ounce of his strength into trying to force it shut.

Suddenly, the boy knew what to do. With one last

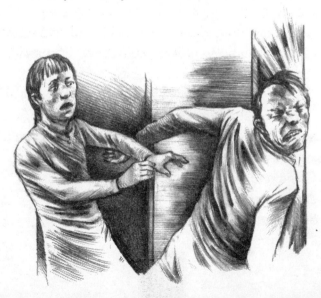

surge he pushed as hard as he could, then suddenly skipped to one side.

The Y'Altai shot out of the broom cupboard like a human cannonball, slammed into the wall opposite with a thud and slumped unconscious to the floor.

* * * * *

'Play for time,' David Tang Snr said to his wife. 'Give them what you can spare.'

'Supplies are running low,' said Mary. 'There's no way we can give them all they want.'

'How have they run down so quickly?' David sounded surprised. 'You should have enough to last for weeks.'

'That's what I thought,' said Mary. 'Seems the master supply programme went down and – ' She was about to tell her husband that for weeks when stores had been logged in at the central supply depot, four times the amount actually delivered had been recorded. The supply officer, thinking he had a glut on his hands, had reduced his orders.

Suddenly Peter Reynolds burst into the room. 'This is an emergency,' he said. 'There's been a burst-out at Nixon Pen, and the prisoners have escaped.'

* * * * *

David tore along the corridor, skidded around one

corner then another and slowed only when he saw another passage cross the one he was in just ahead.

Which way? he wondered as he came to a stop — straight on, right or left?

The way ahead was clear.

So was the corridor going off to the right.

But when he glanced to the left, what he saw set his head spinning.

About ten metres down, the corridor widened into what looked to be a meeting room. In it, obviously in deep discussion, a group of Y'Altais were seated around a table.

Only they weren't all Y'Altais. Even seated, one of the men was obviously a head and shoulders taller than the others.

David recognized him at once.

Sergio Ceraulo.

CHAPTER 14

David's stomach churned with fear as he tried to work out what to do. He daren't try to get into the passage facing him or take the one on the right in case he was spotted.

And he couldn't go back in case the Y'Altai had regained consciousness.

As he stood there, his heart pounding, he noticed for the first time that the walls were lined with shelves, each one tightly packed with books.

Suddenly he felt as if something was pressing into his back.

'What on Earth?' he gasped, turning round and seeing a section of the book-lined wall swing out towards him. 'Wow! A disguised door.'

He slid to one side and stood there as the door slowly opened and shielded him from view.

'They're along there,' he heard someone say.

'I hope they're hungry,' another voice said. 'There's enough food here to feed an army.'

The words were followed by what sounded like a trolley being wheeled along the corridor to where Ceraulo and the Y'Altais were sitting.

'Ah, good. Food,' he heard the American say. 'Sit down, you two; we kept your places.'

Trying to make as little noise as possible, David crept into the gloomy passageway on the other side of the door.

Far to his left, David could hear laughter. *No point in going down there,* he said to himself.

To his right, the corridor ran straight for about ten metres and then looked as if it turned sharply at right angles.

As quietly as he could, he made his way towards the turn and was just passing a long table pushed against a wall when the sound of footsteps stopped him in his tracks. Almost without thinking, he threw himself onto the floor and rolled under the table.

Just in time, for no sooner was he out of sight than two Y'Altais turned the corner ahead.

David's heart sank when he saw two pairs of feet stop in front of his face.

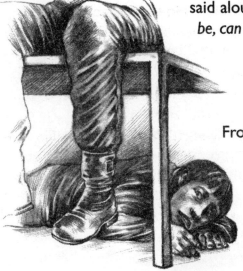

Oh please, no, he almost said aloud, *they can't be, can they?*

But they were. First one, then the other Y'Altai sat on the table. From the way they were swinging their legs, it looked as if they were making themselves comfortable.

* * * * *

'You say you don't trust him, Chi,' said one of the men. 'But he's kept his side of the bargain so far.'

'I know,' said Chi. 'He organized the mass break-out from Nixon. And the Moon's now ours, Ho. Remember that.'

'Or will be when we get rid of the MM people. They're all in Delta 4 now.'

'And it was Ceraulo who gave us the information about the Eutropium.'

'Wonder how he found out about it?'

'When you're running the biggest terrorist organization in the world, there's not much you don't know, I suppose.'

'What's in it for him?' Ho wondered.

'He's part Y'Altai, remember,' said Chi.

'You'd never think it to look at him.'

'His mother must have had the dominant genes, but his father had pure Y'Altai blood in his veins,' Chi said. 'Come on, let's go and join the others.'

As the two men swung down from the table, one of them caught David in the chest with a stray foot.

'Oof!' he gasped, as the wind was knocked from his lungs.

'What was that?' he heard Chi say.

'What was what?'

'That noise.'

'I didn't hear anything. You must be imagining things. Come on, let's go and eat – it smells good.'

'How much longer will there be anything to eat? I wonder,' Chi said as the two men walked towards the door. 'Our fleet won't be here for another two weeks.'

'That's why we're going to attack Delta 4. To get their supplies and make them tell us where their supply depots are. That should keep us going till our people get here.'

'Us and them?'

'Who cares about them?' laughed Chi. 'They can starve to death for all I care.'

'The ones who survive our attack, you mean?' chuckled Ho.

CHAPTER 15

It seemed to take forever before David heard the door at the end of the corridor close and even then he waited for another minute before he dared poke his head out.

'Phew!' he gasped when he saw the coast was clear. He rolled out from under the table.

He ran towards the bend in the corridor and tore round it.

The door at the end was closed. 'Please don't let it be locked,' he breathed, pulling the handle.

'Yes!' he cried aloud as the door opened and he shot through it.

'No!' he breathed a few moments later when he saw two Y'Altais coming towards him. They looked to be so deep in conversation that they hadn't noticed him, but it could only be a matter of seconds before they looked up and saw him racing towards them and a few seconds after that before they realized who he was – and wondered what he was doing.

Just then he saw a narrow passage branch off the corridor. He ran into it so fast that he almost lost his balance and went crashing to the floor, but somehow he managed to keep himself going.

But not for long.

Halfway down the passageway his foot caught the

edge of a rug and he went flying through the air, landing on top of a table that crashed to the floor with a loud splintering noise.

'You all right?' cried one of the Y'Altais, running towards him, obviously thinking David was one of his own.

David sat up and found he was facing a small hatch marked LAUNDRY.

He sprang up and crashed head first through it.

'NOOOOOOOooooooo!' The Y'Altais heard his yell grow fainter and fainter as David tumbled down the laundry chute, turning head over heels and bouncing off one side onto the other.

'This is it,' he thought as he plunged deeper and deeper. 'It's goodbye David Tang.'

But he was wrong, for a moment later he landed with a soft thud in a huge container of dirty sheets at the bottom of the chute.

He lay there for a moment, then clambered out of the basket and looked around, wondering where to go next.

Out of the corner of his eye he spotted an arrow and beneath it the word CARPOOL.

'Thank you!' he cried aloud and tore off in the direction the arrow was pointing. Through one door and down one flight of steps. Along a corridor that seemed to go on for ever. Through two more doors and down another flight of steps and he was there.

He could see his two-wheeler leaning against a

wall, but without his helmet and with no portable life support system he couldn't use it.

He ran from vehicle to vehicle, looking for one with an integral air supply and pressurized passenger cabin.

'Yes! Yes! Yes!' he cried, seeing a Prover parked at the far end of the Carport. 'Please let the keys be inside it.'

He whooped with relief when he saw they were on the dashboard.

He jumped aboard, switched on the engine, rammed the gear into position and roared off, steering a path through the assorted lunar vehicles parked in the Carport.

He was almost at the exit when he heard alarm bells ringing.

Straight ahead he saw a barrier being lowered to block his way.

There's no way you're going to make it! said a voice in his head.

'Watch me!' he yelled, crashing his foot on the accelerator.

The engine roared as the Prover shot towards the exit.

A loud clanging echoed round the cabin as the barrier came down on the Prover's roof, followed a few seconds later by an ear-splitting screech as metal scrunched against metal.

But he made it and, by the time the barrier

touched the ground, the Prover was roaring across the lunar landscape.

Suddenly two dazzling lights flashed into the mirror above the windscreen.

'They're on my tail,' he cried aloud. 'There's two two-wheelers on my tail.'

The landscape on either side became little more than a silvery blur as the Prover flashed along the lunar highway.

Knowing there was no way he was going to shake his pursuers off, David took his foot off the accelerator just enough for the Prover to slow down a fraction and the bike immediately behind to close the gap between them.

When it was less than a metre away, David slammed on the brakes.

The Y'Altai had no chance. He smashed into the back of the much larger and sturdier Prover and a second later his machine exploded in a burst of flame that lit up the land for kilometres around.

'One down, one to go,' yelled David, ramming the

front brakes on.

With a sickening shudder, the Prover spun round 180 degrees.

David's foot came down hard on the accelerator, and the Prover zoomed forward with such power that his arms were almost pulled from their sockets.

Seeing the much larger vehicle thunder towards him, the second Y'Altai lost his nerve and swerved off the highway, his bike weaving wildly across the rocky, dusty terrain.

David could see the Y'Altai desperately trying to regain control, but when his two-wheeler crashed into a large boulder, the doomed driver was thrown off and spun through the atmosphere like a slow-motion yo-yo before landing in a cloud of moondust thirty metres from his burning bike.

'It was only then that David realized that his hands were shaking and his heart was racing wildly. 'Wow!' he gasped. 'Better get back to Delta 4 to face the music.'

'Have you any idea what you've put your mother and me through?' David Tang Snr said for the hundredth time.

David Jnr gazed at his father's weary face on the video link. 'I'm sorry,' he said, also for the hundredth time.

A loud sigh came down the line. 'OK. Tell me again what you heard.'

'I've told you,' groaned David. 'The Y'Altais and the escaped prisoners are planning to take over the Moon. And they're going to attack us for our supplies.'

'When?'

'Dad, I don't know when.' David said the words slowly and deliberately. 'Sooner rather than later, I expect. They've got some supplies but they won't last forever. They'll soon be needing what we've got left.'

'How many are there? Altogether?'

Mary looked at Peter who was sitting alongside her. 'There are 1,500 miners and 300 prisoners.'

'And how many in Delta 4?' asked David Snr.

'750.'

'So they outnumber all of you by more than two to one.'

'I think we can all count,' snapped Mary, then rubbed her brow and said, 'Sorry. I shouldn't – '

But before she could finish what she was saying, her husband's face faded from the screen.

'What's going on?' Peter leaned over to adjust the screen controls. 'Where's he gone?'

'It's all right,' said Mary as the outline of a face came back on screen. 'He's still there.'

But as the face came into focus it wasn't David Tang Snr who was staring at them.

'Good afternoon, Doctor Evans,' a deep, not unpleasant voice said.

'Who are you?' Mary sounded surprisingly calm. 'Where's my husband gone?'

'It's Sergio Ceraulo,' said David. 'The terrorist. You saw him the day you met me at Armstrong.'

'Businessman, please,' said Ceraulo. 'And to answer your second question, Doctor Evans, your husband is still where he was a few moments ago. But as they used to say on television years ago when I was a child, we interrupt this programme to bring you an urgent message.'

'Which is?' Mary asked.

'That Delta 4 is surrounded.'

'And what do you want?'

'Supplies.'

'We don't have much here,' said Mary. 'They're in supply depots in various parts of the Moon.'

'I'm perfectly well aware of that, Doctor,' Ceraulo said. 'I need to know the location of each and every supply depot.'

'You expect me to tell you that?' Mary asked.

'We can wait,' said the American. 'I don't know how many days' supplies you actually have in Delta 4, but – '

'More than enough to last until help reaches us.' Mary sounded very convincing.

Mom could lie straight in an s-bend, David thought, knowing that the supply situation was getting really serious.

'It doesn't really matter how much or how little you have.' Something in the way Ceraulo spoke sent alarm bells ringing in Mary's head.

'Why?' she asked in the same even tone.

'You can have all the food in the world,' Ceraulo sounded amused. 'But without water – '

'You wouldn't!' Mary gasped.

'Even as I speak my men are trying to locate the main pump. And when we find it – I'm sure I don't need to tell you what we'll do when we find it.'

* * * * *

'There's no way I'm telling them what they want to know.' Mary sounded angry.

'What else can we do?' Peter Reynolds was just as angry. 'We've got to negotiate with them at least.'

'Never negotiate with terr – '

Before Mary could finish her sentence, the screen in front of David began to glow. 'There's someone on the videolink,' he cried. 'It's Dad!'

'What happened?' David's father wanted to know. 'One second I could see and hear you all, the next the screen broke up and you'd gone.'

'The Y'Altais and Ceraulo have surrounded the biosphere. They're demanding we tell them where our supply depots are. At least Ceraulo is. And if we don't they're going to turn off the water supply.'

'How long can you hold out for?'

'Four or five days,' Mary replied. 'More if we ration it even more tightly. And if we fill every container in the biosphere, and ration that as well, we can last for about the same again, I guess.'

'Keep going as long as you can,' said her husband. 'The Y'Altais are back at the negotiating table. That's classified. They know we know about the invasion so most likely they'll call it off. In any case, a rescue fleet is getting ready to leave Earth.'

* * * * *

'I'm losing patience, Doctor Evans,' Ceraulo said three days later.

'Not found the main pump yet, Mr Ceraulo?' Mary sounded more confident than she felt.

'The water situation is irrelevant.' Ceraulo smiled. 'You see, when we were searching for the main pump we came across a camouflaged hangar in a crater on *Mare Marginis*. Look what we found inside.'

Ceraulo's face faded from the screen and in its place appeared a sleek, gleaming Starfighter.

'Wow!' gasped David.

'Wow indeed, young Master Tang.' Ceraulo spoke from off screen. 'And it wasn't the only one in the hangar. If someone doesn't tell us where the supply depots are located we'll blast Delta 4 from the face of the Moon.' And with a click, the screen went dead.

CHAPTER 17

Mary keyed in a number on a small videolink set into the top of her desk.

'Yes, Ms Evans?' The Asian whose face came on screen a moment later answered her signal.

'Cochin-Chai.' If Mary was tense there was nothing in her voice that showed it. 'The prisoners have found a hangarful of Starfighters.'

'They can't have.' The colour drained from the Head of Security's face. 'They're in a top-secret location – '

'Built into a crater on the *Mare Marginis*,' Mary interrupted him. 'They found it when they were looking for the main water pump. But that doesn't matter. Why wasn't I told about them?'

Cochin-Chai cleared his throat. 'Their presence here was classified information, graded Double Alpha Plus. Your clearance level is Double Alpha.'

'Why were they here?'

'I'm afraid I can't tell you that.'

Mary's face went white and when she talked, her voice would have frozen the steam in a sauna.

'Commander Cochin-Chai, not only are we running short of supplies, not only have our adversaries threatened to starve us out and cut off our water supplies, they are now in possession of top-secret weapons. I am responsible for the lives of around 750 people, including – ' For a moment there was smile in her voice, '– yours.'

Cochin-Chai's face was ashen. His Adam's apple bobbed up and down in his throat several times before he said, 'Test flights!'

'Testing what? And how big a threat are they?'

'In the right hands, they could nuke a target with pin-point accuracy from a thousand kilometres away.'

'You mean these things have a nuclear payload?'

'They can be equipped with nuclear missiles,' said Cochin-Chai. 'The ones in the *Mare Marginis* are equipped with experimental lasers and other, more conventional weapons.'

'What damage could they do to the biosphere?'

'If they got in close enough and bombarded the same spot over and over again with the new lasers, theoretically they could damage it. That's one of the things we were going to test,' said Cochin-Chai. 'On a disused biosphere on the Dark Side of the Moon. But even if Ceraulo and the others know how to operate them, they won't do any damage to Delta 4.'

'Why not?' Peter Reynolds wanted to know.

'They won't get near enough,' replied Cochin-Chai. 'When they break the heat shield, they'll trigger the automatic laser defence system. They'll be blasted out of the sky before they know what hit them.'

The sighs of relief that rippled round the room were short-lived, for no sooner had Cochin-Chai spoken than one of the other videolink screens glowed and Ceraulo's face appeared in close-up.

'I forgot to tell you when I'm going to attack,' he said.

'Oh really?' said Mary.

'On second thoughts,' Ceraulo smiled, 'perhaps it would be better to maintain an element of surprise.'

'I hope the defence system's as good as you say it is.' Mary turned to the screen filled by Cochin-Chai's face. 'Because I intend to hold out till help arrives from Earth.'

'Oh, that reminds me,' said Ceraulo. As Mary hoped, he had overheard what she had said. 'I'm afraid we had a mishap when we were testing one of the

Starfighters.'

'Mishap?' Mary arched an eyebrow.

'We were testing the laser weapons and one of my men had a little accident with your Earth satellite communication system. I'm afraid he blasted it out of the sky.'

Mary spun round in her seat and told the main communications network to switch to emergency systems.

'Emergency systems inoperable,' the tinny voice told her.

'He's taken out the back-up satellite too,' Peter Reynolds whispered. 'We're completely cut off from Earth.'

David was on an observation deck at the very top of the biosphere when the attack was launched eighteen hours later.

They were the longest eighteen hours of his life. Not knowing when Ceraulo was going to attack was like living on a knife edge.

At first everyone had tried to carry on as normal but soon tempers had started to fray and more than once Security had to be called to break up fights that erupted over nothing at all.

With all mining operations suspended for several days by now, Mary had put everyone to work on routine maintenance tasks in the biosphere with the result that there wasn't an electrical system that hadn't been checked and checked again, not a window that hadn't been cleaned and cleaned again, not a floor that hadn't been scrubbed and scrubbed again and not a vehicle that hadn't been stripped down and re-assembled twice, three times even.

And now there was little to do but wait.

Many took to their sleeping quarters and stayed there writing e-mails to family and friends back on Earth.

Fights broke out in the viewing rooms over which film to watch.

'I never knew grown men could behave like kids,' Peter Reynolds said to Mary.

'Worse,' she managed to laugh. 'And talking of kids, you don't know where David is, do you?'

'Cochin-Chai took him to an observation deck at the top of the 'sphere.'

'Let's go find them.'

Mary and Peter made their way through one deserted corridor after another towards the elevator and up to Cochin-Chai's personal observation deck.

'Hi, Mom. Peter,' said David when they emerged from the lift. 'It's amazing up here. Look at the view.'

Mary looked down. Far below she could see large clusters of red dots and smaller ones of black, easy to spot on the silvery moonscape.

'The red ones are the Y'Altais,' David pointed to the ground far below. 'They wear red space – '

'Look!' cried Mary before he could finish. 'A Starfighter. Coming in to attack.'

It was like watching a silent film. Although he could see the Starfighter outside, all David could hear were sharp intakes of breath from the others on the

observation deck as the plane soared over the biosphere before swooping down.

Streams of lasers beamed from Delta 4's automatically triggered defence system.

'Lock on!' Cochin-Chai shouted. 'Surely one of them must lock on to the blasted thing.'

But whoever was at the controls knew how to handle the Starfighter, making it duck and weave its way through the forest of laser beams.

David couldn't help but envy the pilot's skill.

'What'll happen if he gets through and zaps the biosphere shell?'

Cochin-Chai looked away from David's questioning eyes. 'That shell is made to withstand a meteorite shower. But if they go for the same spot time after time, they could crack it.'

'And what would happen then? If the shell does eventually crack?'

'The air will start to escape, altering the pressure balance on the area around the crack, and . . . ' Cochin-Chai's voice trailed off.

'And?' It was David who spoke.

'And,' Mary took up from where Cochin-Chai had left off, 'the air inside will rush outwards, Delta 4 will explode like a balloon that has been pricked by a pin, and anyone not crushed by flying debris will suffocate to death.'

'What's he doing now?' David wondered aloud as the Starfighter swooped low, then hovered over a tiny biosphere not far away. But before anyone could answer his question, a laser shot from the plane and slammed into the little bubble and one by one Delta 4's defence lasers started to vanish from the sky. 'What's happening?' he cried, turning to Cochin-Chai.

'They've taken out the defence system power supply,' the Asian whispered.

'What does that mean?' asked an ashen-faced Peter Reynolds who was standing alongside.

'It means that we're powerless, literally powerless, to stop them.'

'Look!' cried Peter. 'They're coming in to attack. There's one, two, three – '

'Twelve,' counted Cochin-Chai. 'Every fighter in the hangar!'

'Watch out!' Peter screamed as the V-shaped formation of Starfighters shot towards the observation deck. 'They're going to crash into us.'

For a moment it looked as though Peter was right, but when they were so close that David could actually see Sergio Ceraulo in the lead plane, they soared upwards and, maintaining perfect formation, looped back in the direction they had come from.

'Did you see him?' David gasped. 'Ceraulo in the blue fighter at the – '

'They're changing formation,' Mary cut her son short.

Every eye on the observation deck was fixed on the Starfighters as they regrouped into one long line and, with Ceraulo in the lead, zoomed towards Delta 4 at breathtaking speed.

A second later when it was directly overhead, a laser shot from the lead plane and slammed into the dome with frightening force.

A moment after that, the fighter behind zapped a second laser into exactly the same spot, and even as the pilot at the controls took his plane up and away, the one behind was coming to fire yet another beam of destruction at the doomed biosphere.

'What's the point of them destroying the dome?' David yelled. 'If they do that, they'll never find the food depots.'

'Even if they do, they must know that they can't hold out on the Moon forever,' said Cochin-Chai.

'Two things,' said Mary. 'First, they may not be able to hold out, but if they control the Eutropium supplies, they have the best bargaining tool there could possibly be.'

'And second?' David wanted to know.

'I think this is just a dummy run, to show us what they can do if we don't give in,' Mary replied. 'I expect to hear from Ceraulo any second now.'

But as she spoke a loud whoop from David and a roar from her Number Two stopped her in mid flow.

'What the – ' gasped David.

'Where did – ' gasped Peter.

'What's happening?' Mary turned as she spoke.

'It's the rescue fleet,' yelled David. 'Look!'

As everyone on the observation deck watched, row after row of space planes, their lasers blazing, swarmed down from high above the Starfighters.

First one then another Starfighter was caught in their lethal beams and immediately exploded in a dazzling display of sparks that hung in the sky like huge glittering clouds before showering down to the ground far below.

Ceraulo's blue Starfighter soared high above the

rescue fleet then zoomed groundwards, lasers flashing from its swept-back wings. Gasps filled the observation platform as orange beams zapped into three of the rescue mission craft. They spiralled downwards, flames shooting out of the back.

But the men at the controls of the remaining Starfighters must have realized they were heavily outnumbered, for one by one they rolled their planes over and flashed away with amazing speed, leaving the much older rescue mission craft standing.

With one last defiant flash of his lasers, Ceraulo sent another two rescue craft blazing to the ground before shooting off to catch up with the others.

'Jeez!' gasped David, turning to look at his mother. 'Talk about a firework dis – '

As he spoke the lift door behind Mary Evans slid open and when David saw the man immediately behind it he stopped in mid-sentence and felt fear running through his veins.

'David! What is it?' Mary cried. 'You look as if you've seen a ghost.'

'Not a ghost, Mom.' David pointed at a tall, dark figure walking towards him. 'Definitely not a ghost.'

'Then what?' said Mary, spinning round. 'No! It can't be!'

But it was.

CHAPTER 20

'The Y'Altais!' cried David. 'They've got in to the Biosphere – '

The words died on his lips when he spotted who was behind the Y'Altai. 'Dad?' he gasped.

'It's all right,' David Tang Snr said. 'It's all over. The Y'Altais have agreed to hand over the guerrillas who were attacking MM's installations back on Earth. They've signed a peace treaty with all the countries backing the company. We tried to contact you, but – '

'They knocked out our communications system,' said Mary.

'We gathered that,' her husband said.

'But what are you doing here, Dad?' David was puzzled.

'I thought I'd come along for the ride,' his father grinned. 'Because I could!'

'What about the prisoners?'

'The Y'Altais will have them under lock and key by now,' said David Tang Snr. Seeing the puzzled faces staring at him, he went on, 'We found out Ceraulo was planning a double-cross and managed to contact the Y'Altais here after we left the Earth to give them the news.'

'How?' David screwed up his face. 'The communications system was out!'

'We didn't get through to them until we were

close enough to use non-satellite communication links,' explained his father. 'After Ceraulo and the other prisoners had launched the attack.'

'They're in for a surprise when they get back to base,' said Peter Reynolds.

'They'll be back in Nixon in a few hours from now.' David Snr shrugged his shoulders. 'Now come on, let's go eat.'

'Did you bring supplies with you?' asked Mary.

'No.' David shook his head. 'But with what's in the depots – '

'You mean what little there is in the depots,' said Mary.

'– and with what the Y'Altais have stockpiled, there should be just enough to last till the supply ships get here.'

* * * * *

'David! How are you?' Rachel Ashford smiled at him.

'More to the point, how are you?' said David, seeing the faint red mark on her neck where Ceraulo's handcuffs had cut into it all those weeks before.

'I'm fine.' Rachel ran her hand around her throat. 'You've been having an exciting time, I believe.'

'You could say that.' David fastened his shoulder harness and seat belt, turned to his father and mother and said, 'Mom. Dad. This is Rachel Ashford.'

'Ambassador Tang. Ms Evans.' Rachel smiled. 'Still no sign of Ceraulo?'

Mary shook her head. 'No, they rounded up the nine others as soon as they landed. But he must have suspected something and shot off.'

'Hasn't the thing he's flying got a detector device?' asked Rachel.

'It has,' said David. 'He's neutralized it. He could be anywhere.'

'Well, I hope he's caught soon.' Rachel shivered. 'I hate to think of that madman out there with a Starfighter. I hear he's a brilliant pilot.'

'Best in the United States of the Two Americas' Air Force, before he turned terrorist,' said David's father.

'Don't worry,' Mary smiled reassuringly at Rachel. 'We'll get him.'

* * * * *

Defeat had pushed Sergio Ceraulo's mind over the edge.

In the three days since his attack on Delta 4 had been thwarted he had been hiding out in a small crater on the far side of the Moon listening to curious voices in his head telling him to get even. *No matter what it costs,* they said, *get even. Attack something. Anything. But attack.*

The word stuck in his head. *Attack! Attack!*

And even as the Spacebus with David and his parents aboard was roaring down the runway, Ceraulo was clambering into the Starfighter's cockpit, the word still ringing through his mind.

* * * * *

It was David who saw it first.

As he looked out of the window and saw the Armstrong Lunar Base getting smaller and smaller below, a flash of blue against the black sky caught his eye.

Somehow, maybe because they had just been talking about Ceraulo and the Starfighter, he knew at once what it was.

'Dad!' he screamed at the top of his voice to make himself heard against the roar of engines. 'It's Ceraulo. He's attacking.'

* * * * *

Sergio Ceraulo laughed as he got the Spacebus in his sights, and his thumb rested on the laser control ready to unleash the fighter's lethal weaponry as soon as the craft was in range.

But David hadn't been the only one to spot the Starfighter.

Far below, it had appeared on Cochin-Chai's screens the moment it had come around from the

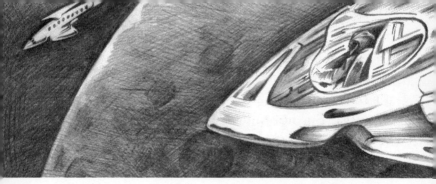

far side, and even as Ceraulo took his fighter closer
and closer in to the Spacebus, Cochin's stealth attack
craft were scrambled hot on the trail.

'5,000 metres and closing,' the computer's
metallic voice echoed round Cochin's control room.

'How far is Ceraulo from the Spacebus?'

'One minute away.'

Cochin-Chai did a quick calculation in his head.
'It's too close to call. Ceraulo will have the SB in his
range the moment we have him in ours.'

Time seemed to stand still as every eye in the
Control Room was fixed on the screen.

'Ceraulo's closing in,' Cochin-Chai's first officer
said without a trace of emotion in his voice.

'Thirty seconds . . . Twenty seconds . . . Ten
seconds . . . Nine . . . Eight . . . ' the computer droned
on mechanically.

'Come on!' groaned Cochin-Chai, gazing at the
screen in front of him.

'Seven . . . Six . . . Five . . . '

'He's accelerating, sir.'

'Four . . . Three . . . Two . . . '

'We're not going to make it, sir.'

'Spacebus in Starfighter's range.'

'Is he in ours?'

'Almost! But not quite.'

Cochin-Chai was not an emotional man, but there were tears running down his face.

* * * * *

Far above, Ceraulo chuckled wildly to himself as he got ready to press the laser control button. Then he paused. 'No hurry,' he chortled, imagining the panic on board the Spacebus. 'Let 'em swea – A-A-AAAGH!'

The stealth attackers' lasers slammed into the Starfighter, blasting it from the sky.

* * * * *

'Honestly!' groaned Jerry Spiller, David's best friend in school. 'First day back and what does she give us for homework? An essay on "What I did during the holidays". Does she think we're in first grade or something?'

'It's not that that bothers me,' sighed David.

'What does, then?'

'It's got to be in by Friday!'

SCI-FILES

THE MOON

The Moon, with a diameter of only 3,456 kilometres, is about a quarter of the size of the Earth and has a mass about one-eightieth of the Earth's mass. It has no weather, air or visible water. Its surface is covered with loose dust and rocks and is pitted with craters.

MAN ON THE MOON

In July 1969, Neil Armstrong and Edwin 'Buzz' Aldrin became the first humans to walk on the Moon.

Since 1972, there have been no manned missions to the Moon, but during the twenty-first century it is certain that people will return there to find out if there are mineral reserves worth mining, to build observatories and to prepare for our next great adventure in space – manned flights to Mars.

LUNAR OBSERVATORIES

In the story you have just read, David is desperate to go to the Blairdome Observatory to watch an eclipse of the Sun. There are already plans to build observatories on the Moon. Why? Because the Earth's atmosphere blurs what is seen through a telescope's lens pointed into space. The near-vacuum on the Moon offers a fantastic location for telescopes.

GRAVITY

The Moon has so little mass compared to the Earth that its gravitational pull on objects on its surface is very much less. A high-jumper who leaped a metre on Earth could jump a clear six metres on the Moon.

NASA and other space agencies are already examining ways of creating artificial gravity. This means that when humans do live on the Moon, the pull of gravity within their bases may feel more like that of the Earth.

GETTING ROUND THE MOON

The crew of Apollo 15, which landed on the Moon in August 1971, were the first to use a Lunar Roving Vehicle (LRV), or 'lunar rover'.

Like all lunar astronauts, the men who drove that LRV had to wear pressurized space suits at all times when they were on the Moon. But scientists at NASA are now working on developing a Pressurized Moon Rover known as a 'Prover'. When people eventually go to live and work on the Moon, they will be able to drive without having to wear space suits.

MINERALS ON THE MOON

NASA already know that many of the minerals on the Moon contain high levels of oxygen. Ilmenite, for example, is a black ore made up of one molecule of iron, one of titanium and three of oxygen. Basalt yields oxygen and silicon.

Plans are already underway to exploit these minerals, by 'cracking' them (breaking them down to their individual components), probably in a solar-powered furnace.

THEIR MASTER'S VOICE

When the story opens, David is telling the master computer, ELVIS (ELectronic Voice-Initiated System), which files he wants to download on to his micro. Voice-activated computers are already in existence.

The transporter that David's mother owns is also voice-activated. Again, this is no longer a fantasy – a prototype voice-activated car was displayed at London's motor show in 1998.

THE PRICE IS RIGHT

In the early days of passenger air travel, flying was extremely expensive – a luxury only the rich could afford. Today, thousands of people travel by air every day.

NASA envisages the same thing will happen with commercial space flights, as spaceplanes become bigger and more economical to run.

LASERS

The first use of lasers as a weapon was demonstrated in the 1960s, but even though billions of dollars have been spent in developing a usable laser weapon, none that we know of has been produced as yet.

The reason why they are, or will be, such highly prized weapons is that they emit energy that travels at the speed of light. The energy from a laser is highly concentrated. The laser beam will be able to cover thousands of kilometres in the blink of an eye to burn a hole in the skin of an enemy spacecraft.

SPACE HOTELS

When David is preparing for take-off on the Spacebus, he mentions to Rachel Ashford that he has been in a space hotel. NASA scientists are not alone in predicting that within the next 30 years, at the latest, these will be in orbit.

The hotels will be much larger versions of the space stations that have already been launched into orbit. NASA predict that space hotels will orbit the Earth 500 kilometres above its surface. Advanced versions of today's space shuttles, known as spacebuses, will ferry guests to and from them.

BIOSPHERES

If we are ever to colonize the Moon, we will have to build sealed environments in which humans can live without having to wear space suits.

NASA sees lunar settlements taking place in three phases.

The first will be what scientists call a 'pod' phase, when lunar living quarters – more or less the same as today's orbiting space stations – will be landed on the

Moon to be used by scientists and researchers.

Next will come the 'hamlet' phase when the space stations will be developed into tiny villages, perhaps linked to one another. They will probably be made of some materials mined on the Moon and others shuttled in from Earth.

As time passes, these hamlets will grow into villages and the villages into towns.

The colonies will be housed in vast domes known as biospheres or ecospheres – totally sealed, self-sustaining systems complete with independent air supplies. Men and women who live and work in them will be able to breathe and move around as normally as if they were on Earth.